HOLLY BLOOM'S GARDEN

Written by Sarah Ashman and Nancy Parent
Illustrated by Lori Mitchell

Flashlight Press

New York

A special thank you to the Lipson Family, Susan, Barry, Elle, Ian, and especially Lainey, for posing for the book.

Copyright © 2004 by Flashlight Press
Text copyright © 2004 by Sarah Ashman and Nancy Parent
Illustrations copyright © 2004 by Lori Mitchell

Printed at Hemed Press, Israel.
First Edition – April 2004.

Library of Congress Control Number: 2003116494

ISBN 0-972-92250-4

Editor: Shari Dash Greenspan
Graphic Design: The Virtual Paintbrush
Title Design: Dean Mitchell
This book was typeset in Adobe Garamond.
Illustrations were created using black Prismacolor pencil and acrylic paint on Arches hotpress watercolor paper.

Distributed by Independent Publishers Group

Flashlight Press • 3709 13th Avenue • Brooklyn, NY 11218
www.FlashlightPress.com

To both Howards, big and little; to Ron and Michael and, of course, to the original Holly Bloom.

– Sarah Ashman and Nancy Parent

I dedicate this book to my mom, Snip, who has encouraged me to draw ever since I could hold a crayon.

– Lori Mitchell

HOLLY BLOOM felt as grouchy as the thorns on a rosebush.
No matter how hard she tried, she couldn't make her flowers grow.

"Don't worry, Sweetpea," said Holly's mother, Iris.
"Some people, like some flowers, take longer to bloom.
They're called late bloomers.
Keep trying. Your flowers will grow soon."

Bud

Rosie

Holly

"I'll plant a garden for you," said Holly's older sister, Rosie,
who had not been a late bloomer. Rosie's flowers were
famous all over town.

But Holly did not want Rosie to plant a garden for her.
She wanted to plant her own.

What I really need, thought Holly, is a green thumb.
Mama says people who can grow flowers have a green thumb.

So Holly took out her paint box,
mixed together some blue and yellow paint,
and gave herself a green thumb.

Then she went outside and planted some new flowers.

But Holly's green thumb disappeared before dinner.
And her dahlias drooped before she'd even had dessert.

Maybe fertilizer would help, thought Holly.

But the fertilizer tickled Holly's nose and her sneezes blew it all away.

Her brother Bud said, "You need to find the right tools."
So Holly looked in the shed.

First, Holly tried a hoe.
She worked until she'd made a perfect patch of dirt.
Then she dug some holes in the ground with a trowel.
Into each hole she put a flower.

Holly filled a watering can and carried it back to the garden to give her flowers a little drink. But the watering can was so heavy she accidentally soaked them.

In the morning, Holly ran to the window
to check on her flowers.
Her daisies had wilted and her petunias looked pathetic.

"I guess I didn't use the right tools," thought Holly,
going back to the shed.

"What's up, Ladybug?" asked Holly's father, Harold.

"I want to grow flowers like Mom and Bud and Rosie,"
Holly said, "but I don't have the right tools."

"Hmmm," said her father. "There are many different kinds of tools.
You just need to find the ones that work for you."

Holly nodded, but she didn't know what other tools to try.

Holly walked sadly through the garden
looking at all the pretty flowers that her mother,
sister and brother had planted. Their bluebells
were brilliant, their gardenias were glorious and
their daffodils were simply dazzling.

Wherever Holly Bloom looked
someone else's flowers were blooming.

That night, Holly's parents tucked her into bed.
"Good night, Ladybug," said her father, kissing Holly on the forehead.
"Sleep tight, Sweetpea," said her mother, turning off the light.

But Holly wasn't ready to sleep.
She had thought of a way to make her garden grow.

When everyone had gone to bed, Holly tiptoed into
her father's art studio. His brushes and paint tubes were
all over the room, but Holly found what she needed
in the special corner her father had made for her.

Holly worked in the studio all night without making any noise.

In the morning, Holly's father put breakfast on the table while her mother arranged some snapdragons in a vase.

"Wake up, Holly! Time for breakfast!" her father called.

Holly's muffled voice came from inside her father's studio. "Just a minute," she replied.

"Holly!" her mother cried. "Were you in there all night?"

"Come on out, Ladybug," said her father with a grin.

Slowly the door opened and there stood Holly Bloom, surrounded by flowers. Oh, what a garden she'd grown! There were tissue paper tulips, crepe paper chrysanthemums and pipe cleaner pansies. Her flowers were made of paper and paste and sparkles and paint. They were full of life, and guaranteed to last forever.

And best of all,
they were grown
especially by
Holly Bloom.